For Mama u Papá

With special thanks
to everyone at David & Charles

First published in 2000 by
David & Charles Children's Books,
Winchester House, 259-269 Old Marylebone Road,
London, NW1 5XJ

Text and Illustrations © Simone Lia 2000

The right of Simone Lia to be identified
as the author and illustrator of this work has been
asserted by her in accordance with the
Copyright, Designs, and Patents Act, 1988.

A CIP record for this title is
available from the British Library.

ISBN: 1-86233-260-6

Printed and bound in Belgium

Billy Bean's Dream

Simone Lia

David & Charles
Children's Books

Billy Bean had a dream.
His dream was to build a
rocket and blast himself
into space.

He drew his rocket and folded it
so that it flew like an aeroplane.

To Billy's surprise, two yellow jellybeans appeared.

"Hello," they said. "We found your rocket design."

"It bumped into my friend's head," said one.

"Shall we help you to build it?" said the other.

Billy was very pleased,
but he told them he had
nothing to build the rocket with.

So Billy was even more surprised when three red jellybeans arrived carrying useful things.
"We heard you talking," said one.
"So we brought these things to help you build your rocket," said another.

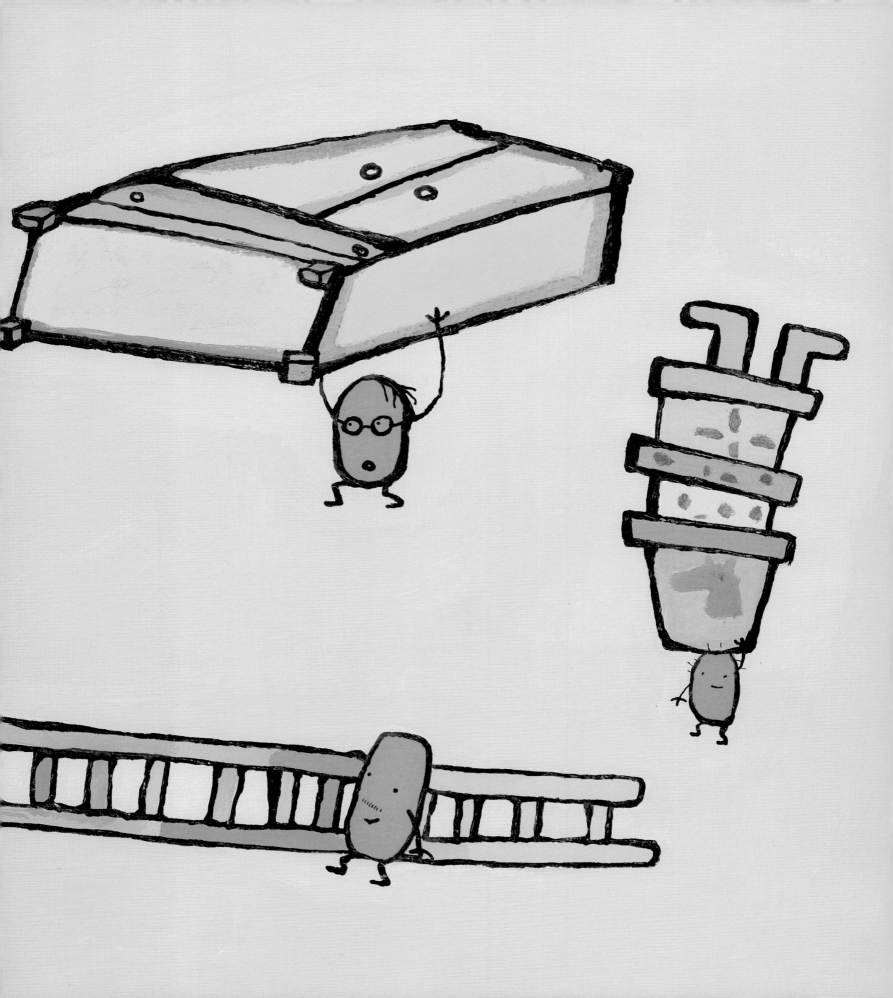

Billy was happy that everyone
was being so helpful.
One of the jellybeans
called his cousins
so they could bring
more useful things.

And soon four green jellybeans arrived and they brought five purple pets with them. There was lots of work to be done.

5 purple pets tried out the rocket seats.

4 green jellybeans sawed wood and hammered nails.

3 red jellybeans made sandwiches.

2 yellow jellybeans planned the journey.

And 1 blue jellybean was very pleased that his dream was coming true.

After lots of hard work, the rocket was almost ready – although some jellybeans argued about whether the rocket should be painted yellow, red or green.

The jellybeans fixed the rocket onto its launch pad, pulling the elastic tight, and loaded it up with their supplies. Then they all climbed in.

"Who's going to get out to cut the elastic?" said one.
All the jellybeans started arguing and shouting and calling each other names.
Until one said, "That's enough!" and climbed out of the rocket . . .

. . . and snipped the elastic . . .

5 4 3 2 1
Blast off!

. . . and the rocket
zoomed into the sky.

That jellybean was Billy.
He watched his dream
machine fly far away.

BUT

Billy Bean was pleased that
he was not in the rocket because
he'd forgotten to pack his pencil
and book. He needed them
because he had a new dream.

Billy Bean had a dream to build
a telescope so that he could
watch passing rockets
fly by.